Nurse Sally Ann

Nurse Sally Ann

By TERRANCE DICKS

Illustrated by BLANCHE SIMS

SIMON & SCHUSTER BOOKS FOR YOUNG READERS

Published by Simon & Schuster

New York • London • Toronto • Sydney • Tokyo • Singapore

More adventures of Sally Ann

Sally Ann on Her Own
Sally Ann and the School Show
Sally Ann and the Mystery Picnic

 SIMON & SCHUSTER BOOKS FOR YOUNG READERS

1230 Avenue of the Americas, New York, New York 10020.

Text copyright © 1988 by Terrance Dicks

Illustrations copyright © 1994 by Blanche Sims

Originally published in Great Britain in 1988 as SALLY ANN GOES
TO HOSPITAL by Piccadilly Press in a slightly different form.

All rights reserved including the right of reproduction in whole
or in part in any form.

SIMON & SCHUSTER BOOKS FOR YOUNG READERS
is a trademark of Simon & Schuster.

Designed by David Neuhaus.

Manufactured in the United States of America

10 9 8 7 6 5 4 3 2 1

Library of Congress Cataloging-in-Publication Data

Dicks, Terrance.

Nurse Sally Ann / by Terrance Dicks ; illustrated by Blanche Sims.

p. cm.

Summary: When a new girl at Mrs. Foster's day care center has an
asthma attack, a doll named Sally Ann accompanies her to the hospital
and breaks the rules about coming to life in front of humans.

[1. Dolls—Fiction. 2. Toys—Fiction. 3. Sick—Fiction
4. Day care centers—Fiction.] I. Sims, Blanche, ill. II. Title.

PZ7.D5627Nu 1993

[E]—dc20 92-22075 CIP

ISBN: 0-671-79428-0

Contents

1

The Emergency

It happened in a flash — the way emergencies usually do.

It was snack time at Mrs. Foster's day care center — the high spot of the day. Mrs. Foster and her helpers always served really good things to eat.

Sally Ann and the other toys — Kaa the python, Clarence the elephant, Arthur the tubby teddy bear, Jacko the

7

monkey, and Stella the golden-haired doll — enjoyed snack time too. Usually the younger children would have a special toys' tea party for them outside the playhouse.

Of course the toys couldn't come alive and eat and drink when there were people around. But they usually managed to hide a few cookies and some lemonade inside the playhouse. Then, at night, when children are asleep and toys can come alive, they'd have a special tea party of their own.

Things sometimes got a bit rowdy at snack time, with lots of hungry children fighting for the food. But Mrs. Foster and her helpers usually kept things in order.

It was the last piece of cake that caused all the trouble.

Tom, one of the bigger boys, had his eye on it, but just as he was about to snatch it, a girl named Jane reached out and took it.

Now, normally Tom wouldn't have minded, but he didn't much care for Jane. She was new at the day care center. They were about the same age, and when Jane first arrived, Tom had tried to be friendly, knowing she must feel strange. But Jane, who seemed to be a bit on the grumpy side, had refused to

talk to him, and Tom's feelings had been hurt.

Suddenly he saw a chance to get back at her.

As Jane turned to pour some lemonade for herself, Tom's hand shot out and whipped the piece of cake from her plate. When Jane looked down, her plate was empty — and there was Tom sitting next to her with the cake on his plate and an innocent expression on his face!

All it meant to Tom was a bit of harmless teasing. If Jane had taken it as a joke, he would cheerfully have given the cake back again.

But Jane didn't think it was funny at all.

She called out to Mrs. Foster, "It's not fair, he took my cake!" She turned back to Tom and shouted, "Thief!"

Tom thought that was sneaky, and insulting as well. Snatching up the cake, he yelled, "Come and get it then — tattletale!"

He set off across the room. Jane was right behind him.

Tom dashed across the big playroom, scrambled over the climbing bars,

dodged around the playhouse, ducked under the play table, and set off around the room again.

Jane pelted after him just as fast as she was able, but somehow she just couldn't catch up with him.

The harder she tried, the angrier and the more out of breath she became.

As she got more and more tired and more and more angry, her breath wheezed painfully in her chest and there just didn't seem to be any air in the room.

To everyone's surprise, Jane suddenly sat down on the floor in front of the playhouse, right in the middle of the toys' tea party.

Horrified, Tom turned and ran back to Jane, where she sat, gasping, in the middle of the scattered toys.

Sally Ann saw at once that something was seriously wrong. Jane had landed just in front of her, and Sally Ann could hear her rasping breath and see the alarming bluish tinge of her face.

Mrs. Foster was trying to quiet the excited children. She hadn't fully realized how serious things were.

As Tom knelt down by Jane, he felt a sharp tap on his ankle. He looked down. It was Sally Ann.

She was breaking all the rules by coming to life with so many people around. But Tom wasn't too astonished. He'd seen Sally Ann come to life before, and he knew she was always ready to break the rules for a good cause.

Tom bent down to the little rag doll. "What is it, Sally Ann?"

"Go and get Mrs. Foster right away. I think Jane may be really ill."

Tom turned and ran across the room to Mrs. Foster. She was a plump, motherly looking lady with big round glasses and straggly gray hair. Although she was sometimes a bit of a scatterbrain, she could be perfectly sensible in a real crisis.

She took one look at the gasping Jane and ran to get the special spray Jane's mother had left for just such an emergency.

The spray helped Jane a little, but she

still seemed to be gasping for air. Mrs. Foster decided to take no chances. She ran to the telephone and dialed the emergency number, 911.

After that there was nothing to do but wait. The whole room was silent except for the painful wheezing of Jane's breath. Mrs. Foster sat beside Jane on the floor, an arm around her shoulders to comfort her.

Soon an ambulance turned the corner of the street and pulled up outside the nursery school. As Mrs. Foster watched the paramedics take care of Jane, she stumbled over Sally Ann. Unthinking, she picked her up, so when Mrs. Foster went into the ambulance with Jane, Sally Ann went along as well.

2

Nurse Sally Ann

Naturally, everyone wanted to hear how Jane was getting along. Tom was especially eager for news. He couldn't help feeling that Jane's illness was all his fault.

Mrs. Foster did her best to make him feel better. "You really mustn't blame yourself, Tom. Jane had an asthma attack, you see. She's had them before, though never as bad as this."

Tom shook his head. "If I hadn't gotten her all angry and worn out —"

"Anyway," Mrs. Foster went on, "Jane didn't respond to treatment too well at the local hospital, and they got a bit worried about her. So they decided to transfer her to Saint Mary's Hospital for Children. It's a special children's hospital. I've just phoned them and they say Jane's much better now. We can go and see her soon."

"Well, that's a relief," said Tom. He grinned. "I wonder how she's getting along with Sally Ann."

Mrs. Foster gave him a puzzled look. "What do you mean?"

"Well, you took Sally Ann with you when you went in the ambulance. And since you didn't bring her back . . ."

Mrs. Foster gasped. "Tom, you're

absolutely right. I took Sally Ann to the hospital with us—and what with all the fuss, I left her on Jane's bed."

To Jane the time after her ride in the ambulance had passed in a sort of haze. She could remember being taken into the hospital, being given tests and X rays and medicine, the hiss of the oxygen mask, and the terrible struggle for breath.

She was aware of people talking in low, worried voices around her bed. Sometime after that there was another ambulance ride, another hospital, more tests, more medicine, more treatment. . . . Slowly she found that she could breathe more easily. Soon, worn out by all that had happened to her, she drifted off to sleep.

When she awoke, she was in a six-bedded hospital ward with Sally Ann sitting on the pillow beside her.

Jane blinked and looked around. The ward was bright and cheerful. The children in the other beds were of all ages and sizes, from a tiny baby in a crib at the far end to a teenager older than Jane. But most seemed to be around the toddler stage.

"Where am I?" muttered Jane.

A clear little voice beside her said, "In St. Mary's Hospital for Children. You weren't doing so well at the local hospital, so they brought you here."

Jane, still a little dazed, rubbed her eyes. "I feel much better now."

"I should hope you do," said Sally Ann briskly. "People were fussing over you most of the night—oxygen treatment, water mist, and I don't know what else."

Suddenly Jane realized that she was having a conversation with a rag doll.

"You can talk!" she said in astonishment.

"Of course I can talk," said Sally Ann. "All toys can come to life when they want to, we're just not supposed to do it when you humans are around. Still, since this is a bit of an emergency . . ."

Suddenly Sally Ann flopped back on the pillow as a pretty, young nurse came up to Jane's bed. "Feeling a bit better now?"

The nurse stayed to chat with Jane for a little while. She told her about Shona, a girl of Jane's own age who had been very ill but was almost well. "Perhaps

you could go and talk to her. You might cheer each other up."

The nurse gave her some more medicine and fruit juice to wash it down, saw that she was comfortable, and then went away.

Jane looked down at Sally Ann. "But how did you get here?"

Sally Ann came to life again and explained. "After Mrs. Foster left me on your bed, everyone assumed I was your very favorite toy, so I got taken everywhere you did."

"Well, you're not my favorite toy," said Jane rudely. "I think dolls are soppy."

"Some dolls may be soppy," said Sally Ann. "But *I'm* not. And you're not my favorite child, come to think of it. You're selfish and rude, for a start."

Jane wasn't used to being talked to like that. Before she could reply, Sally Ann went silent. Jane's mother hurried into the ward, loaded down with grapes, flowers, and candy.

"My poor dear, how are you? Are you feeling better now? I've just had a nice talk with your doctor. She says you've responded very well to treatment and you can come home before very long, once they've done some more tests."

"Are you coming to live in the hospital with me?" asked Jane eagerly. "Some mothers do, the nurse was telling me."

Her mother smiled and shook her head. "I asked, but the doctor said you'd be home so soon, it just wasn't worthwhile."

"Yes, of course," said Jane. "I'll be all right."

But she felt very angry and disappointed all the same.

Soon two more visitors appeared, Mrs. Foster and a worried-looking Tom.

At the sight of Jane's mother Tom looked even more worried, and he apologized for what had happened at the nursery.

Jane's mother was very nice about it, and Tom started feeling better.

But as soon as her mother started chatting with Mrs. Foster, Jane just couldn't help taking her bad temper out on Tom. "It was all your fault, you stupid boy. Now I'm stuck in here. The only good thing about it is at least I'm missing my stupid new school."

Mrs. Foster half heard this last bit and said vaguely, "Don't you like your new school?"

"No, I don't," said Jane fiercely. "And I don't like your silly little after-school club either."

There didn't seem a lot to say after this, and soon Tom and Mrs. Foster brought their visit to an end.

"I pity Sally Ann being stuck in the hospital with *her*," said Tom as they went down in the elevator.

Mrs. Foster smiled. "Sally Ann is a very unusual doll. I wouldn't be too surprised if she ended up doing Jane quite a bit of good."

They reached the main entrance, and Tom paused to admire the two enormous teddy bears standing at the sides of the door. He'd seen them on the way in, and he still couldn't believe his eyes.

They were absolutely huge, bigger than a grown man. The darker of the two wore a red coat and scarf, and his name was Henry. The other was more honey-colored with bigger ears and eyes. His name was Scott. They stood guard at the entrance like two giants of old.

Tom couldn't help wondering if they could come to life like Sally Ann and the other toys at Mrs. Foster's. That would really be something to see, he thought.

Jane's mother left to go back to work. When she'd gone, Jane lay back on her pillows feeling tired and angry.

The teenager they'd seen earlier came up to Jane. "Hello, my name's Helen," she said. "How are you feeling? Is there anything I can do for you?"

"Yes, you can leave me alone," snapped Jane, and Helen went off looking hurt. Somehow Jane's anger changed into sadness, and her eyes filled with tears.

Sally Ann jumped to her feet and stood staring down at her, hands on hips. "This won't do, my girl," she said sternly. "This won't do at all!"

3

A Surprise for Sally Ann

"What won't do?" sobbed Jane.

"You won't," said Sally Ann. "Not the way you're acting at the moment. Why are you so nasty to everyone?"

"Because everyone's nasty to me. And I'm so unhappy."

"What about?" asked Sally Ann gently.

"Oh, everything. Having asthma is

bad enough. Then on top of everything, we had to move here."

"Had to? Why?"

"Dad was out of work for quite a while. Then he got a new job, a really good one. But it meant we had to move."

"But getting a new job was good news, surely?"

"Not for me," said Jane fiercely. "I had to leave my home and my school and all my friends. Mom had to get a job as well to help pay for things, so I have to go to the after-school club at Mrs. Foster's. How would you like to start all over again in a new place with new people?"

"I did," said Sally Ann calmly. "When I first came to Mrs. Foster's, I felt just like you do. But I settled in, and now I'm happier than I was before. That's what you've got to do too — make a new start."

"But I don't know how," said Jane helplessly.

"Just listen to me and I'll tell you," said Sally Ann. She was still talking earnestly as Jane drifted off to sleep.

A little while later Jane woke up feeling rested and called a passing nurse

over to her bed. "I think I feel a little better now. Can I get up for a while?"

"If you're sure you feel up to it. Not for too long now, mustn't overdo it."

The nurse helped Jane into her bathrobe and slippers and she sat on her bed, wondering what to do next.

"Go over and talk to Helen," said Sally Ann. Clutching Sally Ann, Jane went over to Helen's bed.

Drawing a deep breath, Jane said, "Helen, I'm sorry I was so grumpy before. Do you think you could show me around?"

"Yes, of course," said Helen with a smile. "And don't worry, we all get a bit crabby at times." She stood up. "Well, here's the ward. It's quite small, as you can see—just six beds. The patients come in all shapes and sizes."

She led the way out into the corridor. Like the ward, it was brightly decorated, with posters and children's drawings.

On each side, doors led into the various rooms. Helen pointed. "If you go down the corridor and turn right, it takes you into the intensive care area. Children who aren't sick enough for intensive care but aren't quite well enough for the wards stay in those rooms."

A woman was coming out of one of the rooms, calling back to a little girl who lay tucked up in bed, "You're sure then, Shona? Maybe next time, then."

As she closed the door, Jane caught a glimpse of a little girl lying still in the bed, staring into space.

Helen said, "Still no luck, Mrs. Green?"

The woman shook her head. "Not yet. Still, we'll keep trying."

She went off down the hall.

"Who was that?" asked Jane.

"Mrs. Green, one of our play leaders. She's very worried about Shona, the little girl in that room."

"Why, is she very ill?" asked Jane, thinking this must be the girl the nurse had told her about.

"Well, no," said Helen, "that's the strange thing about it. She *has* been very ill, though, five operations in one year. There were all sorts of things wrong with her throat and her breathing. But the operations were all very successful and she ought to be getting better."

"So why isn't she?"

"Nobody really knows," said Helen sadly. "It's as if all the illness and operations and time in the hospital have worn her out. She doesn't even want to play, though Mrs. Green keeps trying." Helen sighed.

"Anyway, come and see our playroom," she said. She led Jane to a brightly decorated room at the end of the corridor on the left.

They watched TV for a while, and then played a game of checkers. After that Jane started feeling tired and went back to bed.

She couldn't help thinking about Shona. Jane looked through the corridor window into the room as she went past. Shona was still lying there, staring blankly at the ceiling. A battered old teddy bear with a red bow tie lay

neglected in the corner. To Jane it seemed that even the bear looked sad.

Jane suddenly realized that other children, like Shona, were much worse off than she was. She wondered if there was anything she could do to help.

It was nearly midnight and the ward was quiet and still. Not completely quiet or completely still, of course. Hospitals never really sleep.

From her place on the end of Jane's bed, Sally Ann could see the other children sleeping quietly. Jane was sleeping too, occasionally muttering in her sleep. Every now and again a night nurse would look in and check up on the sleeping children.

This was the magic hour, the time when most toys come to life. Usually at this time Sally Ann would be enjoying a chat with her friends at the day care center.

She wondered if hospital toys came to life as well. It must be hard for them, she thought, with humans around all the time, day and night.

Suddenly Sally Ann saw a flicker of movement at the end of the ward.

Most of the children had brought at least one of their favorite toys with them. They sat like Sally Ann on the ends of beds, or abandoned on the floor.

But not any longer.

The hospital toys were on the move.

Sally Ann watched as a doll jumped down from the bed of a sleeping toddler and made for the door, followed by a furry toy dog and a shiny rubber duck. A teddy bear and a donkey followed.

Five toys, thought Sally Ann, one for each child.

Suddenly Sally Ann realized—she was the sixth!

Something was going on at Saint Mary's, thought Sally Ann, and she was going to find out what.

She followed the little line of toys out of the ward.

4

The Council of Toys

Sally Ann was never quite sure whether it was luck or magic, but there was no one around as the toys trooped along the corridor.

From the playroom, more toys came out to join them—a shabby tiger, a pony, a lion, and still more teddy bears.

They made their way out of the ward area and into the main corridor, where

They were, of course, Henry and
Scott, the two teddy bears from the
entrance hall.

Some toys took seats at or on the big
table, and the rest crowded around as
best they could.

In a deep, rumbling voice the lighter-colored of the two bears said, "If I may declare the meeting open, Dr. Henry?"

In an even deeper voice the dark brown bear said, "Please do, Dr. Scott."

"Then let us begin. Reports, please. Dennis?"

An old, gray donkey stood up and said, "My child, Maria, is all better and will be going home tomorrow."

There was a little ripple of applause.

The donkey said gruffly, "I'd just like to say how much we appreciate all your help, Dr. Henry, and yours, Dr. Scott."

The bears nodded graciously and Dr. Scott rumbled, "Next."

A woolly monkey stood up and bowed. "My little boy, Peter, is over his operation, and doing well. He tends to rush around too much and tire himself out."

"You must try to influence him to calm down," said Dr. Henry. "Next!"

One by one the toys stood up, reporting on the children in their care, from the very ill to the almost well. Dr. Scott and Dr. Henry gave advice on how the children could best be helped.

At last a teddy bear with a red bow tie stood up. He moved very slowly, and his voice was tired.

"I am still very worried about my little girl, Shona. Her operations have been successful and she should be getting better. But she takes no interest in life and she even refuses to play."

A shocked muttering went around the crowded room.

"Refusal to play is a very bad sign," said Dr. Scott.

Dr. Henry said, "You must try to influence her to play again, Edwin.

Otherwise she may never get well at all."

"I've tried," said Edwin desperately. "I've tried my hardest but she just doesn't respond. And, of course, now that I'm not being played with, I'm fading away too."

"I know it's hard for you, but you must do your best," said Dr. Scott. "We will all try to use silent influence to help you."

Sally Ann scrambled up on a chair and jumped up onto the polished table. "I'm sorry, but I just don't think that's going to work."

There was a gasp of astonishment from the crowd.

"And who are you, young lady?" asked Dr. Henry severely. "And who is your child? Please report in the proper way."

"I'm Sally Ann and my child's name is Jane, bad asthma attack but responding well and making a good recovery," said Sally Ann rapidly. "One or two behavior problems, but I'm working on that as well.

"Now, getting back to Shona, I was there when my child discussed her with another one who knows the case well. Shona is really low, and only strong measures will work."

"I'll try anything," said Edwin.

"Just what are you suggesting?" asked Dr. Scott.

Sally Ann turned to Edwin. "If you want Shona to play, you'll have to ask her yourself."

Edwin was shocked. "You mean, like this? Let her see me when I've come to life?"

"Exactly! Just as you are now!"

Dr. Henry said firmly, "According to the rules, we toys are allowed to use only silent influence on the children in our care."

"What's more important?" asked

Sally Ann. "Keeping the rules—or helping Shona get better?"

Fierce arguing broke out among the toys, and the two giant bears got up and came together, talking in low, rumbling voices.

Then Dr. Henry held up his paw for silence.

"My colleague and I have been considering this case very carefully," he said in his deepest and most serious voice.

Dr. Scott said, "We find ourselves in complete agreement. Sally Ann is right.

This is a case for desperate measures. Edwin Bear, you are hereby authorized to let Shona see you alive as you are now, and to persuade her to play. Sally Ann, you may assist him."

Sally Ann grabbed the astonished Edwin by the paw. "Come on, back to the ward. There isn't a moment to lose!"

Helplessly, Edwin let himself be dragged away.

Little Shona was roused from a deep, sad sleep by a furry paw tapping her on the shoulder. A familiar voice was saying, "Wake up, Shona. Wake up!"

She opened her eyes and saw a teddy bear, her very own Edwin Bear that she'd had since she was a baby, standing on her bed. A rag doll stood beside him. Shona decided she must be dreaming. Still, it was a nice dream.

"What do you want?" she asked.

"We want you to come and play with us," said the doll. "My name is Sally Ann. And this is Edwin, your very own teddy bear. Come and play with us!"

"I can't play," said Shona sadly. "I'm too sick."

"You've been sick," said Edwin Bear. "Very sick for a very long time. But that's nearly over. Now you're more sad then ill—and the medicine for sadness is play."

"Toys need to be played with," said Sally Ann. "We're of no use if we're not. We just fade away. We need you just as much as you need us. Come and play with us, Shona."

"Come and play," echoed Edwin Bear. "You don't want me to fade away, do you?"

He sounded so sad that Shona said, "All right, I'll come and play with you. Not now, though, I'm too sleepy. Tomorrow."

"Tomorrow," said Sally Ann. "Is that a promise?"

"Yes, I promise," whispered Shona sleepily.

Through half-closed eyes she saw Edwin and Sally Ann dance a little jig. "Tomorrow, tomorrow, tomorrow," their voices chorused, and Shona drifted into sleep.

The next morning the doctor came around to see Jane and told her that she could go home that very afternoon. Jane knew her mother would be worried about taking more time off from work, so she asked one of the nurses to phone Mrs. Foster and ask if she could pick her up. Mrs. Foster agreed and said she would let Jane's mother know.

When they were alone, Jane hugged Sally Ann. "Aren't you glad? I shall miss my friends on the ward, though. But I'll come back to see them."

"That's the idea," said Sally Ann.

"I wish I could do something for poor Shona," said Jane. "But I suppose there's no time now."

"Don't you be too sure," said Sally Ann. She told Jane what had happened in the night.

"But," she added, "it wouldn't hurt if you tried too."

Jane hurried to Shona's little room and found Shona still in bed, staring at the ceiling.

"Wouldn't you like to get up and play for a while?" she asked.

Shona just shook her head.

Jane picked up Edwin Bear and held him up. "Your bear wants to play." She held up Sally Ann. "And my rag doll."

"Perhaps I should get up," said Shona, half sitting up. "But I feel so tired, I'm just not sure."

"Oh, come on, try," said Jane.

Somehow, in her determination to help Shona, she forgot her own troubles and was feeling quite cheerful.

That afternoon Jane was all dressed and ready to go. She and Sally Ann were sitting in the playroom so that her bed could be made up ready for another child.

Sally Ann was looking anxiously at the playroom door.

Time was running out.

Shona lay in bed, thinking hard.

She'd awakened feeling sad and hopeless as usual. Then Jane's visit reminded her of her dream.

Or had it been just a dream?

She could hear happy sounds from the playroom across the hall.

She seemed to hear other voices as well.

Voices saying, "Promise . . . tomorrow, tomorrow, tomorrow."

Tom burst into the playroom, dragging Mrs. Foster by the hand. "Here we are, Jane," he said excitedly. "Are you really better? Can you really come home?"

"Of course I can," said Jane. "And so can Sally Ann. I'm sorry I was so mean to everybody."

Suddenly the playroom door opened, revealing a little figure in a nightgown.

A passing nurse looked into the play-room in amazement. "Shona! How nice to see you in there! Are you feeling stronger?"

"It was the toys," said Shona solemnly. She held up the teddy bear in her arms. "My bear, Edwin, and that doll there, Sally Ann. They said they wanted me to come and play with them."

The nurse picked her up. "Of course they did—and so you shall!"

The delighted nurse hugged Shona, Shona hugged Edwin, and Jane was so pleased that she hugged first Mrs. Foster, who was puzzled but pleased, then Tom, who was pleased but embarrassed.

"All right, all right," whispered Sally Ann in her ear. "Now, can we please go home?"

On their way out they passed the two giant teddy bears, Henry and Scott, back in their places by the entrance.

Sally Ann was almost sure that Scott gave her a wink of approval.

The doctors and nurses had a very big job to do, thought Sally Ann. Not to mention the toys.

As they walked out into Summer Street, Sally Ann wished for a return to health for everyone in the hospital for children.

About the author

After editing scripts for the *Doctor Who* television series for six years, Terrance Dicks went on to write fifty *Doctor Who* books based on the program. In addition, he has fifty children's books to his credit, including the Goliath series, *Sally Ann on Her Own*, *Sally Ann and the School Show*, and *Sally Ann and the Mystery Picnic*. In recent years he has worked as a script editor and producer for the BBC Classic Serial.

Terrance Dicks lives in London.

About the illustrator

Blanche Sims has illustrated many books for children, including all the titles in the Kids of the Polk Street School series by Patricia Reilly Giff, *Joey's Head* by Gladys Cretan, and all the titles in the Sally Ann series.

Blanche Sims lives in Westport, Connecticut.

DATE DUE

DEC 2 1 1994			
JAN 7 19 **MAY 4 1998**			
APR 2 8 1995			
JUL 2 6 1995			
AUG 8 1995			